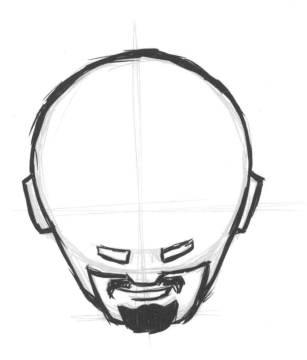

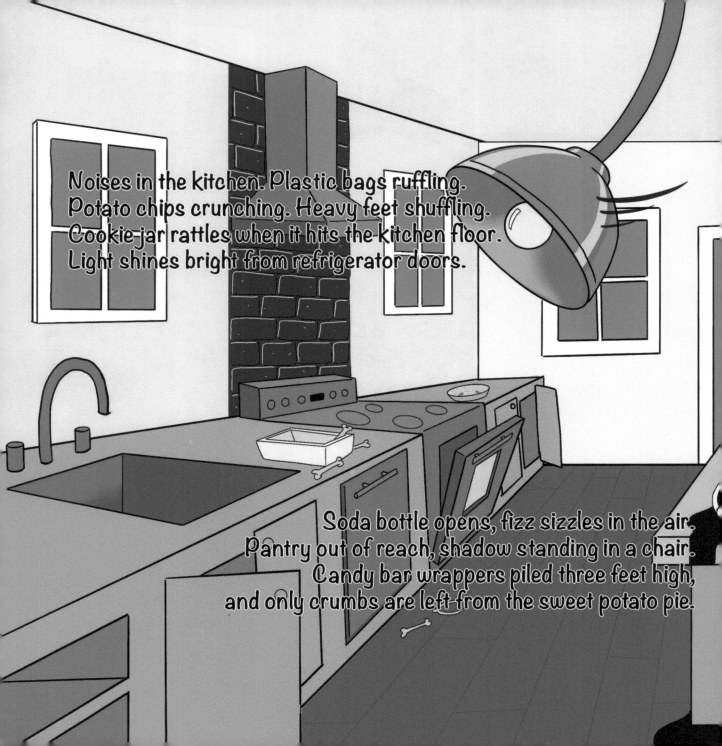

Noises in the kitchen. Plastic bags ruffling.
Potato chips crunching. Heavy feet shuffling.
Cookie jar rattles when it hits the kitchen floor.
Light shines bright from refrigerator doors.

Soda bottle opens, fizz sizzles in the air.
Pantry out of reach, shadow standing in a chair.
Candy bar wrappers piled three feet high,
and only crumbs are left from the sweet potato pie.

The kitchen looks like it survived a tornado.
Nothing left to eat but lettuce and a tomato.
Open chicken boxes, with nothing but the bones,
and melted ice cream drizzled out of broken cones.

It could have been a feast for a big hairy beast,
but footprints in the grease lead out to the streets.
Walking down the block, while he bopped to a beat,
was Snacks with a backpack of junk food to eat.

Like any school day for Tracey and Lil Shawn,
the beams from the sun wake them both like an alarm.
Before she leaves the bed, Tracey stretches then she yawns.
Her brother watches sports until Daddy says "Shaaawn."

Smells from the kitchen lead them both downstairs.
On their plates: egg whites and turkey bacon in pairs.
Wheat toast, jelly, and fruit cut up in slices.
Tracey: almond milk. Shawn: orange juice, ice-less.

Daddy has his pineapple protein shake,
but he has to take it with him, so he won't be late.
He walks Shawn and Tracey to the corner of the block,
says, "Have a good day," when they get on at their stop.

Tracey waves goodbye, Lil Shawn is too cool.
The bus pulls off to take them both to school.
Kids laugh and play and sing songs along the way,
then a donut hit a girl in the head, she yelled "Hey!"

Snacks is in the back with a large half and half.
Juice shoots out of his nose, the donut made him laugh.
Tracey rolls her eyes, "That was NOT cool"!
Then the bus drops the kids off at school.

Its Friday, so Lil Shawn has a test.
He can't wait for gym class and recess.
Tracey paints a picture of sunflowers in art,
then the class gets distracted by Snacks and loud farts.

Half of the class laughs. Tracey shakes her head.
The teacher gets so angry, her face turns bright red.
She storms out the class, but Snacks can move fast,
he runs down the hall and knocks over the trash.

Dashes in the bathroom, tries to catch his breath,
pops a donut in his mouth -- the last one left.
Then the bell rings, everyone gets out of class.
Snacks makes a mad dash to the lunch room... CRASH!!!

Big Shawn hits the gym, today he does squats.
Then he hits the court, puts up a couple shots.
Sips from his shake, wipes his sweat, takes a break,
takes a call from Kasey -- she just left the lake.

Shawn leaves the gym and drives to Kasey's lab.
She has all types of gadgets he can have.
A brand new helmet he taps so they can talk,
and night vision to help see better in the dark.

Back at the school, the lunch room is crazy!
Good food today, no meatloaf and gravy.
Tracey and her friends couldn't even find a seat,
because Snacks took three tables in the back just to eat!

Pizza, tater tots, chicken nuggets, cookies...
it's no way he could eat all that, could he?
BUURRRRP! The sound was like thunder.
His classmates looked for a table to hide under.

BURRPP

He picks up the table, throws it at the door,
then slips and falls in the juice on the floor.
Girls start laughing. It makes Snacks mad,
so he gobbles up all the food the kids had.

"Stop eating so much junk and pay attention.
You could be an A+ student, not to mention,
you could play a sport on the field , or the court,
run and jump with your friends, go outside, build a fort."

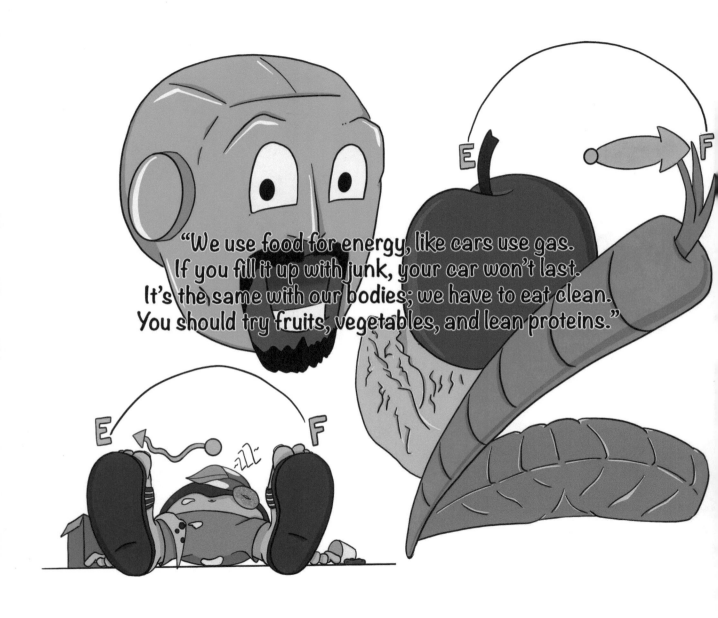

Snacks throws the rest of his junk in the trash,
gives Mr. Powers a pound, then goes back to class.
Teachers are amazed to see a hero in the school.
The principal even makes new Mr. Powers rules.

RRRRIIIINNNNGGGG!!!!

The school bell rings, class is dismissed.
Tracey runs to Lil Shawn to tell him what he missed!
He didn't believe her, they went outside,
and Daddy was there so they could skip the bus ride.

"Guess what? Today Mr. Powers came to lunch!
He set Snacks straight and didn't use his powers once!
I wish you could have seen him! He was so cool!"
Daddy just smiles as they drive home from school.

POWER'S POINT

It's a lot more to life than candy, cookies and pies.
Eat healthy, drink water, don't forget to exercise.
Stay active, then you'll have room for a treat.
Remember eat to **LIVE**, don't live to eat.

CPSIA information can be obtained
at www.ICGtesting.com
Printed in the USA
BVHW020354290922
648251BV00001B/3